STORIES ABOUT ROSIE

STORIES ABOUT

ROSIE

by CYNTHIA VOIGT

illustrated by Dennis Kendrick

ATHENEUM   1986   NEW YORK

For Rosie, of course

Text copyright © 1986 by Cynthia Voigt
Illustrations copyright © 1986 by Dennis Kendrick

Atheneum
Macmillan Publishing Company
866 Third Avenue, New York, NY 10022

Text set by Linoprint Composition, New York City
Printed and bound by South China Printing Company, Hong Kong
Typography by Mary Ahern

10 9 8 7 6 5 4 3 2 1

Library of Congress Cataloging-in-Publication Data

Voigt, Cynthia.   Stories about Rosie.

SUMMARY: Four humorous adventures seen through the eyes
of Rosie, an irrepressible and frisky dog.
[1. Dogs—Fiction.   2. Humorous stories] I. Title.
PZ7.V874St   1986   [E]   86-3640
ISBN 0-689-31296-2

CONTENTS

ROSIE AT HOME

Rosie's home had Daddy and Mommy and Jessie and Duff. Inside, it had an upstairs and a downstairs and an attic and a cellar. Rosie could run upstairs and downstairs whenever she wanted. Somebody had to take her to the attic and the cellar. She couldn't stay there alone, either, because the door would close and then it was dark.

Outside, Rosie's home had a yard with a fence to keep people out. After the fence, there were more yards and houses and streets.

The family's job was to take care of Rosie.
They filled her bowl with water. They gave her
breakfast, every morning, always late. They
opened the door for her to go out and they took
her for rides in the car. They said hello to her in
the morning, when she licked them and their eyes
opened. They said goodnight and scratched behind her ears before she went to bed.

Rosie had her own bed in Jessie's room. She
had the bed by the window. Her bed was exactly
like Jessie's, only it smelled better. When Rosie

was home alone, she jumped up on her bed and looked out the window.

Down below, things moved. She needed to bark at them to say, "Hello. You better go away. Who are you? I'm Rosie."

Rosie barked at her family too. When they came home from school, she would bark. "Hello, hello. I'm Rosie. You're home." When they left, she would run to the window and bark. "Hello. Don't go. Good-bye. Take me with you."

Sometimes, when Rosie barked at him, Daddy said, "I *live* here, you silly goose."

"She's not a goose, she's a spaniel," Duff told Daddy.

Jessie said, "Be quiet, Rosie."

Rosie just barked, "Hello. Hello. I'm glad."

Duff liked Rosie's bark. Sometimes he would bark back.

"Hello," Rosie would bark. "Hello, I'm Rosie, I'm barking."

Duff answered her, but he barked in a way that made no sense. That didn't matter.

"Hello, hello, hello," Rosie barked.

Next door, a lot of things needed barking at, all day. To do that, Rosie ran downstairs and put her head out the window. When somebody walked up to that house, Rosie barked, "Hello, I'm home." When somebody walked away, Rosie barked, "Hello. Go away. Who are you?"

Sometimes, when Rosie looked down from her window, she would see the mommy from next door carrying bags. "Hello," Rosie barked, "Is that something to eat? I'm Rosie. I'm up here. Hello."

The mommy from next door would look up. "Jump, Rosie, jump," she would say.

"Hello," Rosie would answer and run downstairs to bark from a closer window.

One day, Daddy said, "Rosie only barks when people go in or out next door. She doesn't bark when somebody knocks on *our* door."

"Maybe Rosie wants to live next door," Mommy said. "Maybe that is her way of telling us she'd rather live with them."

"Is that what you want?" Duff asked Rosie.

"She does *not*," Jessie said. "Do you, Rosie?"

Jessie hugged Rosie and Duff made his roar at her, so she would run into the kitchen and play. Rosie ran into the kitchen. She hit her bowl. Water fell out of it.

Rosie spun around, fast. "I'm playing," she barked. Duff barked and ran after her. She ran into the living room and jumped up on the sofa.

She leaped off the sofa, jumped up on the
armchair and bounced into the dining room. She
ran under the table, then back to the kitchen.
More water fell out of her bowl, all over her. Duff
chased after her. A stool fell over. Rosie barked at
the stool, "Get up. Are you playing? Hello."

Duff fell over too. "Get up," Rosie barked, at
the stool and at Duff.

"Cut it out!" Mommy yelled.

"Stop this terrible noise," Daddy roared.

Rosie looked up at them. She barked, "We
can all play. All, all." All of them put together

couldn't catch Rosie. She knew that and they
knew it. "Let's all play!" she barked. "Play now!"

"QUIET!" they said.

Rosie sat down.

"That's better," Daddy said.

Rosie didn't mind if the game was over.
There was always something else to do next.
Daddy picked up the stool. Mommy picked up
Duff. Jessie mopped up the water. Rosie wagged
her tail and waited. Their job was to make things
happen next.

Story Number Two

ROSIE GOES OUTSIDE

One of the family's jobs was to open the door for Rosie when she asked. "Out," she would bark, and somebody would come to open the door for her. When she was through being outside she would come back to the door. "In," she would bark.

Rosie could run around outside until she met the fence. Then she could run beside the fence. She could run behind the shed, where the weeds grew tall. She could run to meet Tootsie, and then run back and forth. "Hello. I'm Rosie. You better not try to come in here," she barked.

Tootsie stayed still while Rosie ran back and forth. "Don't move. Go away!" Rosie barked.

Tootsie hissed. Tootsie lived next door, but sometimes she sneaked into Rosie's yard. Rosie liked to have Tootsie in her yard because then she could chase Tootsie out.

In her yard, Rosie could run around in big circles, around the peach trees, around the apple tree, around the holly tree and the lilacs and then back around the peach trees, fast.

When she was tired of running, Rosie could eat an apple. Eating an apple was more fun than eating breakfast. Breakfast just lay there in the bowl, but the apple seemed to want to play.

The minute Rosie put her paws on the apple, it bounced away. Rosie jumped on it. It ran away. Rosie caught it in her mouth. Sometimes that stopped it. But sometimes the apple jumped out of her mouth and ran away again.

She growled at it. The growl tickled in her chest and rumbled out. She growled again.

Her growl scared the apple so it stayed quiet

while she ate it. Apples tasted better than peaches. Rosie didn't like peaches. They never ran away, and when you bit them they were fuzzy. The family's job was to keep the apples there for Rosie and to throw away the peaches and to keep the gate closed so nobody could come in.

When Rosie wanted to go out beyond the fence, she had to be extra smart and extra fast. She had to slip out the front door just exactly when someone came in. If a new friend came to visit Duff or Jessie or Mommy-and-Daddy, Rosie slipped out.

One day, someone opened the front door. "Hello," the family said. "Look out for—"

Rosie wriggled around the legs, fast, and jumped down the steps.

"Rosie!" they called.

"No!"

"Rosie, come back here!"

Rosie ran across the grass and across the street.

"Rosie, come!"

"Rosie, sit!"

"STOP!"

Rosie explored, while her feet ran. Outside the fence, there were other animals and other people. There were clean smells and dirty smells, grass smells and food smells, cars and bicycles

and hills covered with ivy. Rosie was so happy she jumped up in the air. She was happy with all the smells and all the running.

The family ran after her. Rosie ran faster. She turned the corner and ran down the hill. Across the road once and across the road again she ran. Rosie ran and jumped and barked and wondered what would be the next exciting thing to happen.

It was the family's job to run after Rosie. She looked back to be sure they were there and then ran some more, and faster. When she was tired, they would come to get her. They always knew when she was tired. They always knew where she was. The car would drive by and its door would open.

The car stopped beside Rosie.

"Rosie, come," Jessie said. Her voice sounded afraid.

Rosie didn't want Jessie to be afraid. What

was wrong? She jumped up into the car to lick Jessie's face.

"Oh, Rosie," Jessie said. She held onto Rosie's collar and closed the door. Her voice sounded happy then.

Rosie sat in the middle, wagging her tail. Sometimes riding hurt her stomach, but she liked the car.

"Well," Daddy said. He drove the car up the hill and around the corner to Rosie's home. "What do you have to say for yourself, Rosie?"

Rosie was tired and she was thirsty. She was glad they came to get her. She was glad there would be water in her bowl.

Jessie held Rosie's collar all the way from the car to the house. She had to walk bent over to do that, so Rosie hurried.

Rosie drank her water. Mommy gave her more water.

"Rosie, you give me fits," Mommy said.

Rosie wagged her tail and drank her water. Their job was to take care of her. Her job was to be happy.

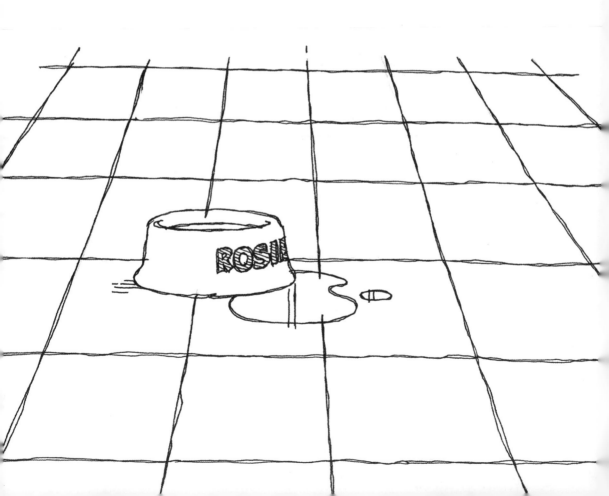

Story Number Three

ROSIE KEEPS THE
BARKING RULE

The rule about barking was easy. Inside the house was for friends. Rosie wasn't supposed to bark at anything inside the house. Rosie had to learn the barking rule.

Once a monster got in the corner of Duff's room. Rosie saw it there. She growled. The monster just stood there. "Get out. Go away," Rosie barked. "Help!"

The monster didn't move.

Rosie barked, to warn them. "Run! It's terrible!"

Mommy came running. Daddy came running.

Rosie barked. "Help! I've got it! Look! Run!"

Jessie and Duff came running.

Rosie barked and barked, so the monster would stay still and not hurt anybody. "They'll fix you. Help! Help! Look out!"

Mommy and Daddy laughed. Jessie and Duff laughed. Rosie barked.

The monster stayed still.

Rosie went up close and barked. "I've got you! Help!" Everybody laughed.

"It's a rug, Rosie," Daddy said.

"Don't tell her," Jessie said.

"Do something!" Rosie barked.

Everybody laughed. Rosie stopped barking. She went up to the monster and smelled it. It was dead. It wouldn't hurt anybody now.

"Good dog," Duff said.

Another time, Rosie went into the dining room and saw a lady on the wall. Rosie didn't know that lady. The lady only had shoulders and a head. She stared at Rosie. Rosie barked. "Hello. I'm Rosie. Go away. Who are you?"

The lady stared and stared.

"You better tell me," Rosie growled. She barked and growled at the lady, so Mommy came in.

"Look!" Rosie barked. She growled, too, to let the lady know that Rosie would take care of Mommy.

"Rosie, that's Grammy. That's a painting."
Mommy picked the lady up and put her on the
living room desk, up high. "You really are a twit,"
Mommy said, scratching Rosie behind her ears.
"But you're right. It isn't a very good painting."

Mommy liked Rosie.

Rosie was smart, so she knew now that she
should only bark at things when they were outside.
She knew she had learned the barking rule.

One night, when Rosie was resting in her
chair, a friend came into the house. This was a
flying friend.

Mommy was correcting tests in the kitchen. "Did you see that?" Mommy asked.

Daddy was watching TV with Rosie. "How did a bird get in?" he asked.

"What are you going to do?" Mommy asked.

Rosie stayed in her chair. She knew the rule now. The rule was, you didn't bark at friends.

Daddy got a broom. Mommy opened the back door. Jessie called Rosie up to her room.

Then Jessie left Rosie alone. Rosie jumped on her bed. She could hear Daddy going upstairs and downstairs. She could hear them talking.

"Bugs are getting in," Jessie said.

"Did you find it?" Mommy asked.

Jessie let Rosie out. Rosie went to sit with Mommy in the kitchen. She lay down on the floor under Mommy's stool. The door was closed again. "I hate birds," Mommy said.

"It's only afraid," Jessie said.

"So am I," Mommy said. "Maybe it's gone back outside."

"I didn't see it go out," Daddy said. He went back to watch TV with Jessie and the broom.

Rosie wanted to go to sleep. Duff was already asleep. The house was quiet.

Suddenly Mommy said, "There it is again!"

She woke Rosie up. Rosie wagged her tail to say hello to the flying friend.

"Which way did it go?" Daddy asked.

"There," Mommy said.

"It's a bat," Daddy said. He took his broom and went upstairs. "I'll check Duff's room. Why isn't Rosie barking?"

"A bat," Mommy said. "A bat!"

Mommy took her tests and put them under the dining room table. Then she sat under the table, correcting tests.

Rosie went to sit with Mommy. Duff sometimes played under the table, but, until now, Mommy never did. Rosie sat up, waiting for what might happen next.

She listened to Daddy. Daddy went up and down the stairs. He went into the attic. He opened doors and closed them. Mommy still sat under the table.

"It's not in my room," Jessie said. She bent down to talk to Mommy. Rosie licked her face.

"I'm going to bed," Jessie said. "I'm going to bed with the door closed. Rosie will keep you safe."

"That's what *you* say," Mommy said. "Sleep well."

"What's the matter with Daddy?" Jessie asked.

"He thinks I'm acting too scared and silly," Mommy said.

Jessie went upstairs. Daddy came downstairs.

"I can't see it," Daddy said. He didn't bend over. All Rosie could see was his legs and the broom. "I don't know where it is."

"I'm sorry," Mommy said.

"I'll have to look upstairs again," Daddy said. "Rosie isn't helping at all."

"I hate bats," Mommy said.

"So do I," Daddy said.

Rosie and Mommy sat under the table.

"Well," Mommy said.

She crawled out from under the table. She went to the kitchen and got a mop. She started to go upstairs. "I'm coming to help," she said.

Rosie went with her.

Mommy went up the stairs like Rosie, on all four legs, only slowly. Rosie was very surprised. The mop clumped. Rosie ran up ahead, then came back to keep even with Mommy. The mop kept on clumping.

Mommy and Daddy poked at the closet in Duff's room, but he stayed asleep. Rosie watched. They closed Duff's door.

They poked in their room, then closed the door. Rosie watched.

They went downstairs. Going down the stairs Mommy put the mop on top of her head. Then they poked at the curtains in the living room and the dining room. Rosie watched them.

They sat down to watch TV. "Anyway, we know it's not in our room or Jessie's or Duff's," Mommy said.

"Some bird dog Rosie is," Daddy said. "Thanks a lot, Rosie."

Rosie jumped back up in her chair and went quietly to sleep. After all, she knew the rule about barking at friends in the house.

Story Number Four

PICKING BLUEBERRIES

The family went to Maine. They took Rosie so they could take care of her there. In Maine, there was a beach to run on. There were islands to explore and rocks to jump over. There were woods to run through and fields of tall grass. Rosie ran in the fields, jumping up to see what was coming next. In Maine, there were shells on the beach and blueberries in the field.

"I'll make a blueberry pie," Mommy said, "if everybody helps to pick the blueberries."

Rosie was glad to help. She ran down the dirt road to the field. The family was slow. Rosie ran back to find them, then she ran back into the big field. On the way back to find the family she followed a rock into the woods. Then she heard them and ran to help out.

Mommy had a big strainer, and so did Daddy. Jessie had her book.

Some crows were already picking blueberries. Rosie ran. "Go away!" she barked, "we are going to eat the blueberries." The birds flew up and flew away. "Hello, I'm Rosie. Come back!"

Daddy said, "I bet if Rosie didn't bark so much, we'd see a deer." He bent over to find blueberries. "She'll scare any deer away."

He dropped some blueberries into his strainer. "I'd like to see a deer," Daddy said.

Mommy sat down to pick. Duff stood right beside her to help. He talked and talked. Mommy picked. She got up and moved to a new place. Duff went with her to help some more.

Rosie went to help Jessie. Jessie sat down and opened her book. "Hello Rosie," she said. "It's a nice day, isn't it?"

Rosie went to help Daddy. She watched his fingers pick blueberries. He bent over and his fingers picked. Rosie opened her mouth and picked blueberries. They rolled down her throat. They tasted good. She picked some more.

"Duff, you aren't helping, you're talking,"

Mommy said. Duff went to help Daddy.

Rosie ran across the field. There might be a crow. There might be two crows or three.

"Jessie, aren't you going to help?" Mommy asked.

"I don't feel like it," Jessie said. "Somehow, I don't feel like picking blueberries. I feel like reading."

Mommy moved to another place and sat down to pick. Rosie sat down with Mommy. "Hello, Rosie," Mommy said. "This is slow work. I'm glad it's not my regular job."

Rosie was glad too. She was so glad, she ran to the edge of the field. Something moved in the woods. She went to catch it. It was a butterfly. Rosie ran after the butterfly.

The woods smelled good. The woods smelled a little bit like the blueberry field and a little bit like the beach and a lot like pine trees and birch trees, rocks and dirt and moss. After the butterfly got tired, Rosie ran through the woods. "Hello," she barked. "I'm Rosie. I'm here. Hello."

She came to a sunny place and stopped. The trees were tall and the rocks were big. Sunlight warmed up the moss and made it smell like wet dirt. It was shady all around, but sunny just there in the middle. The trees made shadows. The shadows moved across the moss.

It was the kind of place where things might happen, the kind of things that can only happen once. Rosie waited.

An animal came up through the trees. It was

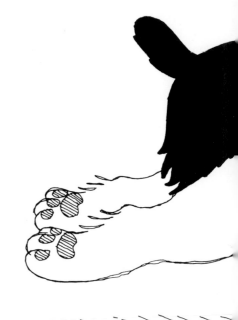

a tall animal, much taller than Rosie. It was as brown as the tree trunks. It walked so softly, Rosie could hardly hear it walking. The animal stood in the sun. The shadows moved on its back.

Rosie had never seen an animal like this. It had antlers growing out of its head. She felt afraid and she felt glad.

Rosie looked at the animal. The animal didn't see her. The animal put its head down to smell the moss.

Rosie didn't even want to bark. She was so glad, her tail wagged. She was so afraid, she sat down and stayed still.

The animal saw her. It turned and ran away, making almost no noise in the quiet woods.

Rosie didn't even run after it. She just wanted to sit for a moment, wagging her tail.

Then she walked back toward where the field was. Seeing the big animal had made Rosie want to walk slowly.

A white moth flew by her face. Rosie jumped
to catch it, but it got away. "Wait!" she barked. "I
can catch you. Hello!"

She ran back to the field. The family was
going away and Rosie ran to catch up with them.

"Hello, Rosie," Jessie said. "Where have
you been?"

"Jessie, you can clean these blueberries for
us," Mommy said.

"Sure," Jessie said. "I like cleaning. I just
don't like picking."

When they got back, Jessie ran water in the sink for the blueberries. Mommy got the pie ready. Duff went to ride his bike. Rosie and Daddy rested. "I'd still like to see a deer," Daddy said.

"There's no chance of that with Rosie around," Mommy said.

"Rosie, you deadbeat dog," Daddy said.

Rosie went to say hello to Daddy. He scratched her head.

"Rosie wouldn't be nice to you if she knew what you were saying about her," Jessie said.

"Yes, she would," Daddy said. He scratched some more.

"Rosie, come see *me*. *I* don't say mean things about you," Jessie said.

Rosie knew that, but she went to say hello anyway.

"Well," Daddy said, "at least my worst fear hasn't come true. I was afraid Rosie would catch a skunk. That would be pretty terrible."

Jessie laughed. Daddy and Mommy laughed. Rosie let them laugh. She knew she had met a deer. Unless it was a skunk she had met.

"I know something you don't know," Rosie barked.

Jessie gave her a blueberry to eat.

"I do, I really do," Rosie barked.

Jessie gave her another blueberry.